Farmer Dray's farm

Apple Tree Station

Apple Tree Village

Church

School

Farmyard Tales

The Naughty Sheep

Heather Amery

Adapted by Anna Milbourne

Illustrated by Stephen Cartwright

Reading consultant: Alison Kelly

This story is about
Apple Tree Farm,

Mrs. Boot
the farmer,

Sam,

Poppy,

Rusty,

Woolly,

some
flowers

and a country fair.

One morning, Mrs. Boot said, "It's the country fair today."

"People show things from their farms."

"The best things win prizes."

Let's take apples!

After breakfast, they picked shiny apples.

Let's take flowers too.

They were so busy, they didn't see the open gate.

Woolly did.

"What's outside this field?" Woolly wondered.

She went to look.

She found a garden
full of flowers.

They looked pretty...

...and they were
tasty too!

Munch!
Munch!

Just then, Rusty
saw Woolly.

Mrs. Boot was
very upset.

They're
ruined!

"I can't take any flowers
to the fair now."

"Never mind,"
said Poppy.

They got their coats
and set off.

Woolly watched them.

She decided to go too.

There were lots of people
at the fair.

Woolly found some
other sheep...

...and a nice man.

Mrs. Boot saw Woolly.

19

It was time to go home.

They didn't win a prize
for apples or flowers...

...but they did win
a prize for Woolly.

Clever, naughty Woolly!

PUZZLES

Puzzle 1

In which order did Woolly
eat the flowers?

A.
- blue
- red
- yellow
- pink

B.
- pink
- yellow
- red
- blue

C.
- yellow
- red
- blue
- pink

D.
- red
- blue
- pink
- yellow

23

Puzzle 2

Choose the right speech
bubble for each picture.

A.

Puzzle 3

Which of these won a prize?

Rusty   apples   Woolly

Puzzle 4

Can you find these things
in the picture?

apples
bird
tree
cat

Puzzle 5

Spot six differences between these two pictures.

Answers to puzzles

Puzzle 1

C.

🧩 yellow

🧩 red

🧩 blue

🧩 pink

Puzzle 2

A.

Let's take apples!

B.

C.

Puzzle 3

Woolly won a prize.

Puzzle 4

tree

bird

cat

apples

Puzzle 5

Designed by Laura Nelson
Series editor: Lesley Sims
Series designer: Russell Punter
Digital manipulation by Nick Wakeford

This edition first published in 2015 by Usborne Publishing Ltd.,
Usborne House, 83-85 Saffron Hill, London EC1N 8RT, England.
www.usborne.com Copyright © 2015, 1989 Usborne Publishing Ltd.

USBORNE FIRST READING
Level Two

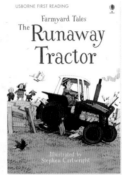

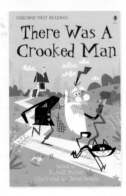

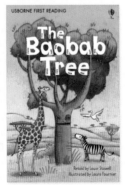